THIS BLOOMSBURY BOOK

BELONGS TO

....

FOR DAD AND MY FIRST BOX OF CRAYONS. NL

FOR LAURA, WHO POINTED OUT THAT OUR CAT SMUDGE
THOUGHT WE WERE HER PET HUMANS - MR

First published in Great Britain in 1999 by Bloomsbury Publishing Plc
38 Soho Square, London W1V 5DF
This paperback edition first published in 2000

A CIP catalogue record for this book is available from the British Library.
ISBN 0 7475 4689 4 (paperback)
ISBN 0 7475 4020 9 (hardback)

Designed by Dawn Apperley
Printed and bound in Belgium by Proost NV, Turnhout.

3 5 7 9 10 8 6 4 2

Rover

Michael Rosen  Neal Layton

BLOOMSBURY
CHILDREN'S
BOOKS

This is my pet human. Humans come in all sizes: she's the kind who is a bit bigger than me.
    I named her Rover.

Her ears are not as good as mine.
She has very weak claws.
Her coat only covers her head.

Her dad, who I call Rex, has coat on his face. Her mum, who I call Cindy, doesn't.

Sometimes I sit on Rover. Sometimes Rover sits on Cindy. Sometimes Rover sits on Rex. Sometimes we all sit on each other.

Rover doesn't eat her food properly.
    She pokes it with metal things.

At night, I take her to her basket. It's very long and when she's in it she hides under a cushion with small bears.

I let her have a rabbit as well, though I would like it in my basket.

Her bark is very squeaky. Sometimes my friends bring over some other small humans. As they're young we think it's all right if they bark a lot together.

When Rover and I go to the park she keeps losing her ball but I always bring it back for her.

She has to spend a lot of time watching a loud, coloured box. When she's bored with it, I wag my tail and she watches that instead.

In the summer I lead them to the family box and Rex and Cindy move it very quickly to the seaside. I help it go faster by putting my head out of the window.

VROOm!

We go to an enormous sandpit where the humans rip off nearly all their winter overclothes. Then some of them run about in coloured underclothes, and some lie down and pretend to be dead.

One day last summer we sat in the sandpit while the wind blew the sand all over us. I liked it but Rex and Cindy didn't. In the end they fell asleep under a blanket.

Near where we were sitting, a man and woman were trying to eat each other.

That was when Rover went for a walk.

I was sad to see her getting smaller and smaller and then disappear.

Then Rex came out from under his blanket. He stood up and looked up and down the sandpit.

Then he woke up Cindy and they both started barking.

Cindy rushed over to the people eating each other and started pointing all over the sandpit and barking some more. Then they all looked at me.

Rex waved Rover's rabbit under my nose and barked at me. It was getting very loud and all the people who had been lying down now stood up. Cindy patted me and Rex waved Rover's rabbit again.

I thought it was time to go back to the box but I didn't want to go without Rover. So, I walked off down the sandpit to fetch her.

Rex and Cindy walked behind me. They kept looking at the sea.
Every human we walked past they barked at.

There was a group of humans who were trying to smash a ball into a net. Sometimes they missed and it went over. Then they barked a lot.

I couldn't see Rover.

Rex and Cindy were breathing loudly and there were more lines on their faces than usual.

Then we got to the rocks. In between the rocks there were puddles. In the puddles there were stupid things with eight legs that walked sideways.

Rex and Cindy wanted to go back and tried to make me come too.

I thought that was a bad idea because as far as I knew we had come to the rocks to get Rover and bring her back.

I jumped over the rocks.

I couldn't see Rover. I looked back and there were lots of people standing at the end of the sandpit waving their arms.

Rex and Cindy were squeezing each other.

Then I jumped over one more rock and there was Rover
staring into a puddle.

I barked. She looked at me and pointed at one of those stupid eight-legged things. I barked again, and Rex and Cindy came over the top of the rock and started barking and howling.

Their eyes were all watery and they rushed up to Rover and picked her up and squeezed her.

Then we headed back. Cindy and Rex kept patting me all over and squeezed my neck. Quite a lot. Rex kept showing Rover's rabbit to everyone and pointing at me.

At last Rover could come in the box too.

And I thought: next time she starts getting smaller and smaller, I'll chase after her to keep her nice and big.

Acclaim for this book

'Layton's wildly exuberant illustrations provide the perfect accompaniment
to the four-legged narrator's refreshing brand of humour and innocent
observations of the world around him' *The Guardian*

'Neal Layton's lively, humorous pictures are just right for the story' *The Daily Telegraph*

'Layton's wonderfully free scribbly pencil and bright wash illustrations are
full of humorous, acutely observed touches that interact well with Rosen's deadpan text ...
children will love this clever, jokey book' *Books for Keeps*

'The doggy descriptions of Rover, her family and her friends are completely hilarious'
The Bookseller